Dedicated to our Beloved

Centurion and Emperador

who are the true inspiration for this book.

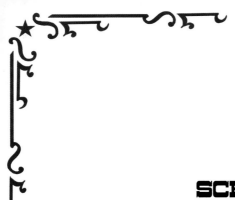

STORY
Rob and Patricia Schneider

SCRIPT
Patricia Schneider

ART
Francisco Herrera

COLORS
Fernanda Rizo

LAYOUT DESIGN
Mike Kennedy

FOR CENTURION & EMPERADOR:
DR. LARRY GALUPPO & EQUINE SURGERY, (RESIDENTS, STUDENTS, AND STAFF)
EQUINE ULTRASOUND FACULTY (FELLOW AND STAFF AT UC DAVIS SCHOOL OF VETRINARY MEDICINE)
DR. VANESSA ROOD, DVM ETAL. (NAPA VALLEY EQUINE)
BILLY RODRIGUEZ & ENRIQUE RODRIGUEZ (RANCHO UVA BLANKA)
MARGARITO HERNANDEZ (RANCHO CENTURION RANCH MANAGER)

CAROLYNNE GAMBLE (CONSULTANT)

PHOTOGRAPHY BY JULIA KUZMENKO McKIM

www.CENTURIONandEMPERADOR.com

MAGNETIC PRESS

MIKE KENNEDY, *President/Publisher*
WES HARRIS, *Vice President*
DAVID DISSANAYAKE, *PR & Marketing*
4910 N. WINTHROP AVE #3S
CHICAGO, IL 60640
WWW.MAGNETIC-PRESS.COM

CENTURION & EMPERADOR
OCTOBER 2016. FIRST PRINTING
ISBN: 978-1-942367-29-1
All content TM and © 2016 GEORGE GAMBLE

WELCOME!

I HAVE HAD THE GREAT PLEASURE AND HONOR OF KNOWING NANCY WHITE GAMBLE AND HER HUSBAND GEORGE FOR ALMOST TWENTY YEARS.

THEIR LOVE AND APPRECIATION FOR THE BEAUTY AND PRESERVATION OF NAPA COUNTY AND NORTHERN CALIFORNIA IS ONLY MATCHED BY THEIR LOVE AND ENTHUSIASM FOR THEIR BRILLIANT AND TALENTED DANCING HORSES, CENTURION AND EMPERADOR.

IT REMINDS ME OF WHAT THE GREAT CHARLIE CHAPLIN SAID ABOUT THE EARLY DAYS OF ANIMATION, "IT'S NOT FAIR! WE ACTORS CAN'T DO THE THINGS THEY CAN!" WELL, I'VE NEVER SEEN A HORSE IN MY LIFE SWAY THEIR HIPS TO SALSA MUSIC OR THE LATEST POP SONGS LIKE CENTURION. IT IS MARVELOUS TO WATCH AUDIENCES ENTHRALLED BY THESE TALENTED EQUINE HOOFERS!

IN SHOW BUSINESS, YOU ALWAYS HEAR ABOUT A GUY WHO CAN DO THIS OR THAT, SO WHEN NANCY CALLED ME TO COME SEE HER NEW DANCING HORSES, WHILE ALWAYS PLEASED TO SPEND TIME WITH NANCY AND GEORGE, I DIDN'T EXPECT MUCH.

I ARRIVED TO WITNESS THE JAMES BROWN OF FOUR LEGGED ANIMALS. CENTURION JUST LOVES TO 'SHAKE IT' AND LITERALLY DANCES HIS HEINY OFF.

THE MORE YOU LEARN ABOUT THE HORSE, THE MORE YOU GET TO APPRECIATE THE JOURNEY HE HAS GONE THROUGH. HE WAS A MISTREATED AND ABUSED ANIMAL. THE PHOTOS OF CENTURION BEFORE THE GAMBLES ACQUIRED HIM JUST BREAK YOUR HEART. BUT TO SEE HIM NOW IN ALL HIS PURE WHITE STALLION GLORY IS A REAL WONDER TO BEHOLD.

NOT ALL ANIMALS HAVE THIS STORY BOOK ENDING, BUT HORSES LIKE CENTURION AND HIS BEST FRIEND, THE MAJESTIC FRIESIAN DANCING HORSE EMPERADOR, DESERVE TO HAVE THEIR STORY TOLD HERE WITH THE BEAUTIFUL ARTISTRY BEFITTING THEM BY MY GOOD FRIEND FRANCISCO HERRERA AND STORY BY THE MULTITALENTED PATRICIA SCHNEIDER.

SO SIT BACK AND GRAB THE KIDS AND GRANDKIDS AND ENJOY THE FIRST EDITION PRINTING OF "CENTURION AND EMPERADOR!"

READ ON!
ROB SCHNEIDER

ONCE UPON A TIME

there was a lovely place called *THE GAMBLE RANCH*.

The Ranch had a rooster, a pig, a sheep, a little mouse and a Mama Duck, who were very well cared for by their owners, Nancy and Mister.

They were all very happy... well, almost everyone.

Mama Duck was sad because she didn't have any ducklings of her own and she wished with all her heart that she could have someone to love and take care of.

One stormy night the sky was filled with giant clouds and soon heavy drops of rain started falling on top of the barn.

A flash of lightning lit up the night sky revealing two storks, Rob and Bob each carrying a heavy sack from their beaks.

Soaking wet and exhausted, they landed on top of the barn, then flew inside through an open window.

Shaking the water from their wings, one of the storks took a scroll from his sack saying: "May I have your attention, please? By the power vested in us as storks in the State of California, we are proud to announce the arrival of two baby horses."

"This is highly irregular!" said George the Rooster, "There was no mention of any babies to be delivered; no mention at all!"

Rob leaned over to Bob and said: "I told you to make a left at the third rain cloud an hour ago, Bob!"

"Well, Rob, I couldn't hear you! We were in the middle of a storm, remember? We're lucky we didn't crash, especially with how heavy these youngsters are!"

Two baby horses peeked out from the sacks.

"Where do I sign?" Mama Duck yelled as she rushed over to the storks.

"No one is signing anything! There are no horses of any kind at this Ranch!" cried George the Rooster!

"Well, now there are!" said Mama Duck, as she grabbed the Stork's receipt and quickly initialed where it said: "Terms and Conditions, No Returns or Exchanges!"

Mama Duck quickly named the baby white horse CENTURION and the baby black horse EMPERADOR.

George the Rooster said, shaking his head: "In the morning, I must Cock-a-doodle-doo this news to Nancy and Mister."

"Welcome to our home, little ones! I'll take care of you!" said Mama Duck.

The next morning, Nancy and Mister opened the barn door and were surprised to find two new members of their ranch.

"Well, what do we have here?" said Nancy. George the Rooster was going to say something, but Mister interrupted. "Welcome to our ranch little ones!" said Mister.

"But we don't have anything fun for them to do here to make them happy," Nancy mentioned with concern.

"Well, there is a race track in town, maybe they can learn to run there, and if they do well, they can become race horses one day. Maybe that will make them happy," said Mister.

With that, Mama Duck kissed the new babies and whispered, "Don't worry, my little horses. You are going to be very happy here." The horses sighed with joy.

Centurion and Emperador grew bigger and stronger every day while running on the town race track. But their running didn't exactly look like the other race horses. They kicked their legs a little too high, and they swayed quite a bit with their hips.

"This is shameful," crowed George the Rooster. "Those two are just not good at running!"

The other young horses in town made fun of them, and didn't let them play their horsey games, like 'Horse' or 'Role Over' or 'Catch Me If You Can'.

"You're not very good at being race horses," they yelled. "Horses run fast and straight and neither of you can do either! Maybe you can find a race where the horses boogie instead of running fast!" They laughed.

Centurion and Emperador were sad, so Mama Duck tried to make them feel better. "Don't let anybody make you feel bad. I love you both and I know in my heart that you two are very special. Listen to yourselves and one day you will find what makes you happy."

The Town Fair was coming and the big attraction was the horse race followed by the fair's very popular Dance Show.

Centurion turned to Emperador with concern.
"I don't want to run anymore. The other horses are right. We aren't very good at racing. I don't want them to make fun of us again in front of all those people. We have no chance of winning."

"We have to keep running," said Emperador. "Maybe we'll get better at it. It's what everyone says we're supposed to do."

"I know. But maybe we can be good at something else? Does running make you happy?" Centurion asked.

"It doesn't matter," said Emperador.
"We're horses. We have to be good at racing."

"Sometimes I get this feeling that we're going to be good at something else. Something special, like Mama Duck said," Centurion said with a sigh. "Maybe something that the other horses can't do."

"Well, until then, we'll just have to race and do the best we can. What else can we do?" asked Emperador.

Finally the day of the big Town Fair came.
Horses from far away came to the town to race.

Nancy and Mister were very excited to watch
their horses race for the first time.

Mama Duck had proudly decorated two beautiful
red capes with their names for the race.

Centurion and Emperador looked
a little anxious.

"Don't be nervous, I am sure you are going to do
just fine. Just do what feels natural," said Mama
Duck to her lovely children.

The race began and the horses took off, but it looked as if Centurion and Emperador had glue on their shoes!

They weren't as fast as the other horses. In fact, some of the other horses were laughing and pointing at the weird way they were running. And so the race ended with Centurion and Emperador tying for last place!

Centurion and Emperador looked at each other sadly. "You were right, Centurion," Emperador said with disappointment. "We're no good at racing. Maybe we're not good at anything."

"I didn't say we aren't good at anything. I just think we're going to be good at something else, something very special! All we have to do is find out what it is!"

They were walking by the arena
when a concerned man ran to the band
and yelled,

"The Dance Show dancers got lost and
they're not going to make it to the Fair!
What are we going to do? Everyone is
waiting for the Dance Show to begin!"

"Let the band play,"
said one of the musicians.
"At least the people can enjoy the
music."

So the band started playing,
but the people were disappointed.

"Where are the dancers?"
they all wondered.

And then, suddenly . . .
Centurion felt his legs moving to the beat of the music.

"What are you doing with your legs?" asked Emperador.

"I don't know, but it feels pretty good!" said Centurion.
"You should try it yourself!"

"I don't think I can, Centurion..."

"Yes, you can, Emperador! YOU CAN DO IT!"

And then, Emperador felt his legs moving, too.

Emperador smiled, and together the two young horses
started dancing to the music!

Centurion and Emperador swayed and shimmied,
stepping to the beat. They bopped and they danced in
the most amazing ways. Their hoofs were in sync and
their moves were spot on as they moved their bodies to
the rhythm of the music!

The other horses were so impressed
that they tried to imitate their dance moves,
but they were race horses without
any rhythm for dance.

When the show ended, Centurion and Emperador bowed.
They knew that the entire audience had been wowed.
They finally found something that they were both very good at!

Nancy and Mister were over the moon with joy to see how much
everyone loved Centurion and Emperador's performance.

Mama Duck whispered to the horses, saying:
"I love you and I am so very proud of you both!
I always knew the two of you
were special!"

CENTURION & EMPERADOR

And so began the adventurous careers of
Centurion and Emperador,
the now famous dancing horses!

CENTURION AND EMPERADOR
A LESSON FROM OUR DANCING HORSES

WE ARE VERY EXCITED AND PLEASED TO INTRODUCE CENTURION AND EMPERADOR, OUR MAGNIFICENT AND TALENTED DANCING HORSES TO THE WORLD!

WE ADOPTED CENTURION IN 2013. HE HAD BEEN ABUSED AND WAS NEAR STARVATION, WITH THE LOOK OF DEATH IN HIS EYES. BUT WITH A LOT OF TENDER LOVING CARE, HE WAS NURSED BACK TO HEALTH. HE KNEW HE FINALLY HAD A LOVING HOME AND A RANCH THAT WAS SO PROUD OF HIM THAT IT WOULD BE CALLED *RANCHO CENTURION* IN HIS HONOR. DESPITE HIS PAST ABUSE, HIS SPIRIT HAD NOT BEEN BROKEN. WE SAW SOMETHING "SPECIAL" IN HIM AND NOW WANT TO SHARE HIS "SPECIAL GIFT" WITH EVERYONE: *DANCING!*

HIS NEW HOME IS NOW FILLED WITH OTHER RANCH ANIMALS, BEAUTIFUL PASTURES, AND THE LOVE AND KINDNESS HE DESERVES. HE IS NO LONGER DEPRIVED OF FOOD, SHELTER, OR LOVE.

CENTURION'S OWN STORY IS ABOUT HOPE, STRENGTH, COURAGE, AND PERSEVERANCE AGAINST ALL ODDS. AS HORRIBLE AS HIS LIFE HAD BEEN, HE NEVER GAVE UP.

BUT THIS STORY OF CENTURION AND EMPERADOR IS ALSO A STORY OF UNCONDITIONAL LOVE, AND THE FAITH THAT THEIR MOTHER INSTILLED IN THEM FROM THE TIME THEY WERE LITTLE -- THAT NO MATTER WHAT, THEY WOULD GO ON TO CONTRIBUTE SOMETHING SPECIAL IN LIFE.

EVEN IF THEY WEREN'T GOOD AT SOMETHING, OR BULLIED BY PEERS, THEY WOULD HAVE THE LOVE AND SUPPORT TO CONTINUE ON AND FIND WHAT THAT SOMETHING SPECIAL WAS. AND THEY *DID* FIND IT!

IT WAS DANCING! THEIR STYLE OF DANCE IS BEYOND COMPARE. WHAT MAMA DUCK PROVIDED FOR CENTURION AND EMPERADOR WAS A MOTHER'S LOVE AND SUPPORT.   AND DESPITE THE BULLYING, SHE TOLD THEM, "YOU CAN DO IT"! AND THEY DID.

TODAY, CENTURION AND EMPERADOR LOVE TO PERFORM, AND THEIR AUDIENCES ARE AMAZED AT THEIR GIFTED AND UNIQUE STYLES OF DANCE. THEY HAVE RAISED THOUSANDS OF DOLLARS AT A CHARITY EVENT IN THEIR OWN COMMUNITY, *HANDS ACROSS THE VALLEY,* WHICH HELPS PROGRAMS FEED THE HUNGRY. CENTURION KNOWS ALL TOO WELL WHAT IT'S LIKE TO BE HUNGRY, AND IS NOW GIVING BACK TO THOSE IN NEED. FOR MANY

YEARS THIS CHARITY EVENT HAS BEEN HONORED BY THE PRESENCE OF OUR DEAR FRIEND **ROB SCHNEIDER,** AND HIS SUPPORT AND GENEROSITY. IT WAS ROB WHO INTRODUCED CENTURION TO JAMES BROWN'S **"GET UP OFFA THAT THING"!** DANCING TO JAMES BROWN, FRANK SINATRA, PHARRELL, ELVIS, MICHAEL JACKSON OR WHOMEVER, CROWDS ALWAYS CALL FOR AN ENCORE AS THEY BOOGIE WITH THE BEAT ALONG WITH CENTURION. CENTURION IS NOW IN HIS GLORY, AND SO ARE WE.

Above (left) Emperador, (middle) George and Nancy Gamble with Centurion, (right) Centurion

WE HAVE BEEN BLESSED IN SO MANY WAYS BY THESE HORSES. IN 2008, NANCY WAS DIAGNOSED WITH A RARE FORM OF LEUKEMIA (ACUTE PROMYELOCYTIC) THAT BROUGHT HER NEAR DEATH. NOW, COMPLETELY CURED, CENTURION HAS BROUGHT A NEW LEASE, LOVE, AND PASSION TO HER LIFE. THEY BOTH SURVIVED THEIR LIFE ALTERING EXPERIENCES AND CAN NOW SAY, "WE DID IT!"

WE ADORE CENTURION AND EMPERADOR, JUST AS EVERYONE WHO SEES THEM ARE AWESTRUCK BY THEIR BEAUTY, STYLE, AND GRACE. THEY ARE LIKE FRED ASTAIRE, MICHAEL JACKSON, AND JENNIFER LOPEZ IN THE WORLD OF HORSE DANCING.

WE HOPE THIS STORY INSPIRES AND GIVES THE STRENGTH, COURAGE, AND LOVE TO ALL CHILDREN WHO MAY HAVE BEEN CHALLENGED IN THEIR LIVES BY THEIR PEERS OR THEIR TALENTS TO PERSEVERE.

GEORGE AND NANCY GAMBLE,
Owners, Centurion and Emperador

Above (left) Rob with Centurion, (right) George and Nancy Gamble with Rob and Francisco

PATRICIA AZARCOYA SCHNEIDER IS A MEXICAN ACTRESS, WRITER, AND THE MOTHER OF **MIRANDA SCARLETT SCHNEIDER,** WHO LOVES HORSES AND HAS BEEN HER INSPIRATION FOR THE WRITING OF THIS BOOK.

SPECIAL THANKS

TO *ROB AND PATRICIA SCHNEIDER* FOR WITHOUT THEIR INSPIRATION, DEDICATION, TIME, TALENT, AND CREATIVITY, THIS STORY OF TWO DANCING HORSES WOULD NOT HAVE BEEN BROUGHT TO LIFE. THE STORY IS BEAUTIFULLY WRITTEN AND THE MESSAGE IS ONE THAT CHILDREN OF ALL AGES CAN BENEFIT FROM. ROB, THE MULTI-TALENTED WRITER-ACTOR HAS BEEN A FRIEND FOR MANY YEARS. PATRICIA HAS SPECIAL GIFTS OF HER OWN AND WRITING IS ONLY ONE OF THEM. PATRICIA AND ROB HAVE COLLABORATED WITH US ON THIS PROJECT AND WE ARE HONORED TO HAVE SHARED OUR LOVE AND PASSION FOR OUR TWO DANCING HORSES, CENTURION AND EMPERADOR, WITH THE SCHNEIDERS.

THIS PROJECT BRINGS AN AMAZING MESSAGE OF PERSEVERANCE AND UNCONDITIONAL LOVE. THANK YOU ROB AND PATRICIA FOR BEING OUR FRIENDS AND WRITING SUCH A TOUCHING STORY THAT WILL INSPIRE AND TOUCH THE HEARTS OF ALL ITS READERS. CENTURION AND EMPERADOR LOVE THEIR STORY AND WILL BE HONORED TO DEDICATE TO YOU THEIR NEXT DANCE.

AND TO *FRANCISCO HERRERA,* OUR NEW FRIEND WHO WAS INTRODUCED TO US BY ROB SCHNEIDER. FRANCISCO IS A WORLD-CLASS CHARACTER ARTIST WHOSE BRILLIANT IMAGINATION, CREATIVITY, AND ARTISTRY HAVE BROUGHT THE STORY AND CHARACTERS TO LIFE. HIS TALENT IS SURPASSED ONLY BY HIS IMAGINATION, WHICH GREW BEYOND OUR VISION. HIS PASSION, ENTHUSIASM, AND DEDICATION HAVE FAR EXCEEDED OUR EXPECTATIONS. FRANCISCO, YOU SAW WHAT WE SAW IN THE STORY, AND YOU TURNED IT INTO ART. WE LOVE IT AND KNOW THE READERS WILL TOO.

THANKS FOR SHARING OUR LOVE AND PASSION FOR THESE TWO GREAT HORSES!

- George & Nancy Gamble